FOR JULIE

my guiding star

—E. V.—

Vacationers
from Outer Space

BY EDWARD VALFRE

chronicle books · san francisco

Once we took a family car trip into the middle of nowhere.

At a rest stop

our journey took

a very unusual turn.

Mom ordered

a cup of coffee.

Who could have known

it was really

a secret window

into another galaxy?

In a flash of light,

a flying saucer

appeared above our table.

Who were they?

Where did they come from?

And most important,

would I still get dessert?

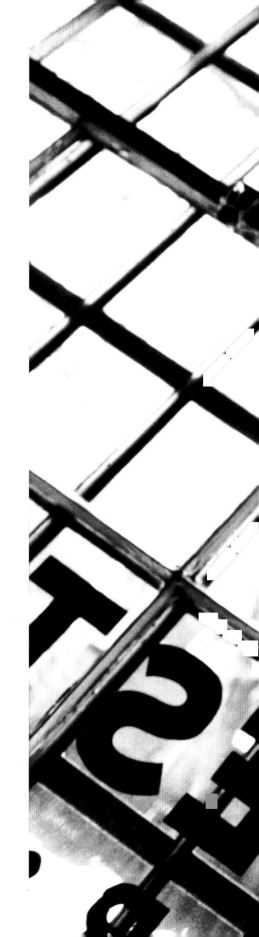

But a buckaroo must always

be ready for adventure.

There was only one thing to do.

According to Article Seventeen,

Paragraph Three of the Buckaroo Code:

When faced with invasion from outer space . . .

Save planet Earth

and try not to get

too dirty.

But I was without
a spaceship and
a space buckaroo
without a spaceship
is like a cowboy
without a pony.

Luckily, this was the
land of used rockets.
There were bubble gum
spaceships for those
long intergalactic flights.

Some could travel at the speed of light.

Others had a sporty moon roof.

I went with the deluxe model complete with

Shortly after blastoff,

we caught our first glimpse of the aliens.

They were asking a cow for road information.

"If you reach the Milky Way,

then you've gone too far,"

I heard her say.

One of my robot scouts

went ahead

to check out the situation.

He returned with

the troubling news

that a nearby town

had been taken over

by aliens.

No time to waste.
A swarm of deadly
space orbs *zoomed*
behind us in *hot* pursuit.
I *leaped* forward,
hit the *hyperdrive* button
and we *raced* away.

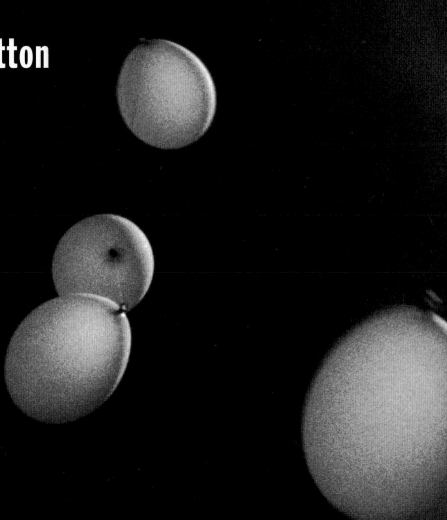

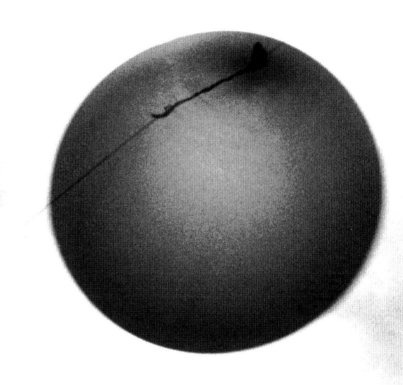

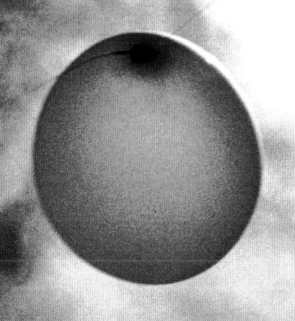

Strangely,
the same button
tuned in to a
country-western
radio station.

To the sounds of a twangy guitar

we managed to land

at a roadside stand.

While Mom and Dad shopped

for astronaut snacks,

I searched for aliens with

my Subatomic Bubblizer 2000.

The local authorities did not believe
my warning about the space invaders.

But my super space buckaroo instincts
gave me the feeling I was being watched.

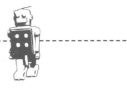

Suddenly a voice from

around the corner whispered,

"Silly silly earthling.

We do not come to invade your planet.

We come for fun."

It was an alien in a clever disguise.

It was over a few root beers

that Glort from the planet Googie 7

told me our world had been discovered from

old television signals floating across space.

Earth was considered one of the greatest

amusement parks in the galaxy.

"Your planet is so minty fresh," he said.

TO TELESCOPE ←

I waved good-bye to my friend from another world

and wondered if our vacations

would ever cross paths again.

Glort was headed to Paris, France.

And we were off to an observatory

high up in the mountains.

An astronomer told me that

all of the stars

and all of the planets

are traveling through space

at incredible speed.

The whole universe

is on one big journey

to nobody knows where.

It's a mysterious universe out there

for a space buckaroo.

And you can discover its secrets

in the stangest places—

even on a family vacation.

Book design by Lisa Lytton-Smith.
Printed in Hong Kong.

Library of Congress Cataloging-in-Publication Data
Valfre, Edward.
Vacationers from outer space / by Edward Valfre.
p.   cm.
Summary: While traveling in his family's sedan "spaceship,"
an imaginative Backseat Buckaroo decodes alien messages,
witnesses a high-speed flying saucer chase, and saves planet Earth.
ISBN: 0-8118-1717-2
[1. Imagination—Fiction. 2. Extraterrestrial beings—Fiction.]
I. Title.
PZ7.V253Vah   1997
[E]—dc21   97-1351
CIP
AC

Distributed in Canada by Raincoast Books
8680 Cambie Street, Vancouver, British Columbia V6P 6M9

10 9 8 7 6 5 4 3 2 1

Chronicle Books
85 Second Street, San Francisco, California 94105

Website: www.chronbooks.com

"Your planet is so minty fresh"

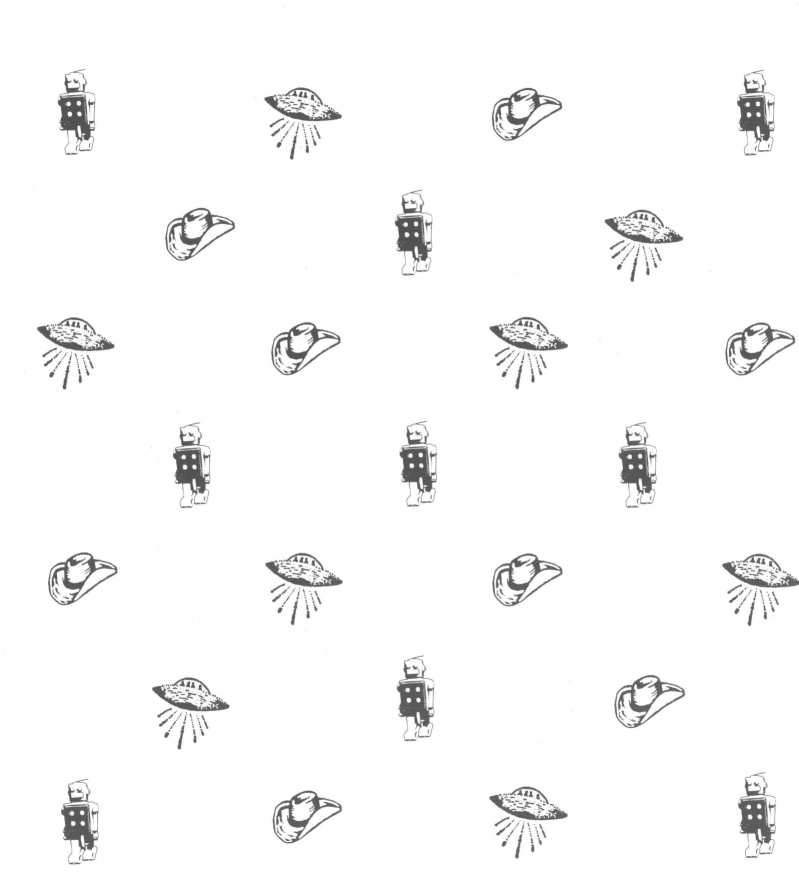